Tombi's Song

Tombi's
Song

by Jenny Seed

Illustrated by Dugald MacDougall

Rand Mc Nally & Company

First published in Great Britain 1966
by Hamish Hamilton Ltd.
90 Great Russell Street, London, w.c.1

Like most little Zulu girls in South Africa, Tombi had her own special song. Her mother had made it up for her when she was a baby, jogging up and down in a blanket tied to her mother's back. It went like this:

Tula umntwane!
Hushaby baby!
Mama's coming!
She's gone to the store
To buy brown porridge.

Tombi was six years old now but she still sang her special song. When she was happy it made her feel even happier, and when she was unhappy —which was not often—it gave her comfort.

This morning Tombi sang her song because she was happy. She was

going to the store to buy sugar for her mother. In her hand she clutched a shiny silver ten cent piece. This was the first time she had been allowed to go all the way to the store on her own or carry precious money, like a big girl.

Skipping and dancing, Tombi ran across the bare, swept ground between her mother's hut and the hut of her grandmother. Still singing, she turned off on to the narrow uneven path that led down the low grassy hill.

All around Tombi were hills, settled comfortably into the earth as if they were drowsing in the dry afternoon sunshine. It was autumn and the silky grass was golden and the day warm and hazy.

Tombi stamped her feet and kicked out her legs and twisted her body so that the skirt of her dusty pink dress went this way and that. She was going to the store all by herself, like a big girl.

"Sabona, Tombi! I see you!"

Tombi stopped and turned round.

"Yebo!" she shouted in reply. "Greetings!"

Coming down the path from the huts on the hill opposite was Zenela, Tombi's cousin, with a cane basket balanced on her head.

"Where are you going, young
sister?" called Zenela while she was
still quite a long way off. "If you are
going to the road you can walk with
me. I am taking this basket to the
stall to sell. Is it not a beautiful basket? I helped Mama dye some of the
grass red and green for the decora-
tion."

9

"Hawu! It is a lovely basket!" exclaimed Tombi in admiration.

Zenela was a year and a bit older than Tombi and she could do many things Tombi could not. She went to school and could write her name on a slate. She could help her mother weave baskets and earn money. She could even balance burdens on her head. More than anything in the world Tombi wished she could be big like Zenela so that she could be her friend.

But Zenela did not think of Tombi as a big girl. She always teased her as if she were a very small child.

"I am going to the road, big sister," Tombi said when Zenela came swinging up to her. "I am going farther than the road. I am

going to the store to buy sugar for my mother." Proudly she showed the shiny silver ten cent piece. "I am carrying a great amount of money."

"Hawu!" laughed Zenela. She had often carried money. The basket on her head was worth much more than ten cents. "Hold tight to such a fortune, Tombi," she teased, her dark eyes dancing with merriment. "You know what the old people say.

Money is slippery. One minute you have it in your hand and the next it is gone. Pshew! It has slipped away!"

Tombi knew Zenela was teasing her but she closed her fingers tightly round the coin. Once when she was younger her grandmother had given her a cent to buy a sugar stick when she went shopping with her mother. She had put it carefully into her pocket, but on the way to the store she had lost it. Somehow it had slipped away. It was true, money was slippery!

She walked behind Zenela on the narrow path, clutching the ten cents anxiously, until they came to the wide main road that twisted and curved between the hills all the way

down the Coast. It was a very busy
road. Cars raced past at great speed,
going to or coming from many holiday beaches.

Some of the cars stopped at the
little stall made from bamboos that
stood in the grass on the side of the
road. The people in the cars bought
bananas or avocado pears from the
big girls carrying tin basins of fruit,
or chose one of the baskets that hung

like weaver birds' nests from bare branches thrust into the ground next to the stall.

"I must stay here to sell my basket," said Zenela. Then looking down at Tombi, she added, "Are you not afraid to cross the busy road? Shall I take you over?"

Tombi was afraid of many things but she did not want her cousin to know. "Why should I be afraid?" she asked. "I am not a small child to be afraid!"

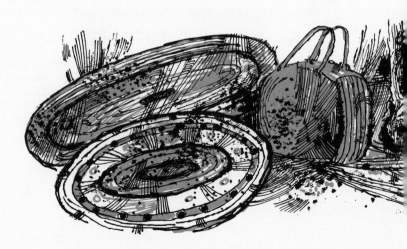

The women sitting in the grass near the stall heard Tombi. They stopped their weaving and threw back their heads and laughed. There was nothing they liked more than a little teasing and fun to help pass the time while their fingers were busy.

"Hawu!" cried one. "Tombi has grown so big! She is no longer a little girl."

"Sabona, little Grandmother!" shouted another. "I see you." This made the women laugh more than ever.

Tombi felt hot with shame. She did not dare to look at Zenela. "I must go on to buy the sugar," she said.

"Be careful, Tombi!" called out a woman who was making a large washing basket. "It is well you are so big or you would be afraid to go through the dark forest."

It was Tombi's aunt who was teasing her now. Tombi looked down respectfully. "Why should I be afraid of the forest, big mother?"

"Oh! Oh! Oh!" said her aunt while the women waited, smiling.

"Do you not know?" she asked, her big eyes opening wide. "The monster ISIQUQUMADEVU, lives in that dark forest!"

The women clapped their hands and laughed with delight. "ISIQU-QUMADEVU! ISIQUQUMADE-VU!"

Zenela was laughing, too. "Go well, young sister! They are only teasing you."

Tombi felt very small. She waited

till there was a break in the traffic, then crossed the main road. She turned down into a sandy road that led to the trading store.

At first there were fields on either side with huts and women hoeing. Then came the forest.

The forest was so thick that no one could walk through it except along the road. It was very dark with tall spreading trees, wild bananas, a tangle of bush, and long trailing creepers and monkey ropes.

The nearer Tombi came, the darker the forest seemed. The empty yellow sand road in front of her looked very lonely.

Tombi did not believe in the monster. "There is no such thing," she told herself. "It is only a story."

The big people often teased children about the monster. They said he was very hideous with a long beard and was so big he could swallow whole villages in a single gulp. They said he hid away in forests waiting to snatch small children, especially when they had been naughty.

Tombi's grandmother had often told her stories about the monster. After she had heard them Tombi would lie awake on her grass sleeping mat for a long time, too afraid to close her eyes in case the monster should come and carry her off.

"Tula umntwana! Hushaby baby! Mama yesa! Mama's coming!"

Tombi sang softly to herself because she did not want to be afraid. She walked down the very center of the road, kicking up the soft, cool sand with her toes. She kept looking into the dark forest. But all she could see were trees.

Then suddenly Tombi stopped. Between the monkey ropes and the twining creepers with purple flowers she could see bright red fruit. African plums! Tombi loved their sweet milky juice and soft tangy flesh.

She ran across the road. She climbed up the bank and crouched down, peering through the under-growth. The light was greenish in the spaces under the trees and the air was heavy with the smell of damp, rotting leaves. The plum bush was laden with fruit but to reach it she would have to crawl right into the forest.

Tombi kept very still and listened. Everything was silent except for the distant twittering of some small birds. There was not even a breeze to stir the leaves. It was as if the forest were watching . . . waiting. . . .

"I see you little girl."

Tombi jumped up with a gasp.

Coming down the road was a woman with a huge bundle of firewood on her head.

"Are you picking the tasty fruit, little girl?" she asked, smiling down sideways at Tombi.

"I should like to," answered Tombi, "but I am on my way to buy sugar."

She was thankful she was no longer alone. Quickly she jumped down on-to the road and walked with the woman till they came to the store.

The trading store was a red brick building with a wide verandah. It was built on the other side of the forest strip. People were standing

about on the steps and walking to and from the holiday cottages on the low bushy hills. Over the hills was the beach and the sea.

Tombi liked going into the store. It was quite dark inside after the bright sunlight, and there was a good smell of new material and bright rubber balls and washing soap and dried beans and flour.

"Yes?" asked the lady behind the long wooden counter.

"Sugar," said Tombi shyly, holding out the shiny silver ten cent piece.

The lady brought out a brown paper packet from under the counter. "Ten cents sugar," she said, taking the money.

Tombi reached for the packet with both hands. She held it very carefully and went out of the store. She turned back up the road into the forest. It seemed darker and more silent than ever.

She looked back to see who else was coming, but this time no one else was coming. She would have to go alone.

"Zenela is not afraid of the monster," thought Tombi, "because she is a big girl. And so am I. I have bought groceries and soon I shall go to school and be able to write my name. Soon I shall be able to weave and earn money. Soon I shall be able to carry burdens on my head."

She walked down the road on the side, quite close to the forest to show she was not frightened. She put the packet of sugar on top of her head and held it there with her hands.

Quite often she had tried balancing things on her head. Things like pebbles or sticks or mud cakes. She had never tried anything as big or as heavy as a packet of sugar. She remembered how easily Zenela had come swinging down the hill with the basket.

Carefully Tombi took her hands away, just a little, from the sugar. She held her head high and her back very straight. She could feel the weight of it, easy and comfortable. Slowly she lowered her arms. She walked with the packet balanced on her head, like a big girl.

Suddenly there was a dreadful noise behind Tombi—a roaring, rushing, snorting, crashing noise! Even before she could turn it was

upon her, screeching and trumpeting so that the whole road trembled.

Tombi threw up her hands in fright. She leapt onto the bank at the side of the road as a swirling yellow cloud of dust thundered past. The sugar fell off her head and dropped with a heavy sound into the loose sand. The paper packet burst open and the white sugar poured out. The sugar! Oh, the sugar!

Tombi lifted her head and stared after the yellow cloud. It was the bus, packed full of laughing brown people, and with bags, boxes, bundles of thatching grass and suitcases tied onto the roof.

After it had hurtled round the next bend with its hooter going full blast, the dust settled down onto the bushes. Tombi sat on the bank and looked at the broken packet. She tried to scoop up the mound of

sugar with her hands but it trickled through her fingers and mixed with the sand.

Her eyes felt very big but she did not cry. Very slowly she stood up and walked on.

How was she going to tell her mother? Money was so precious! Surely her mother would be very sad and there would be no sugar to put in the tea.

If only she could earn money like Zenela. If only she could weave or had something to sell at the stall. She thought of the bigger children standing beside the busy main road, holding out bunches of bananas or basins of avocado pears to the passing cars.

Just then Tombi came to the place

in the forest where the African plums grew. They were so red and luscious. Surely many people would want to buy them.

But they grew in the dark forest— in the bearded monster's forest!

"What if it is not just a story?" thought Tombi quickly. "What if ISIQUQUMADEVU is really hiding in there waiting to snatch me up?"

Tombi crouched down on her haunches and looked once more into the trees. All was so silent, watching . . . waiting . . . She was so frightened she almost turned to run away. But how could she tell her mother there was no sugar? She began to crawl under the bushes.

Branches scratched her and tendrils tangled about her arms and face.

She pushed and pulled and in a moment she was through the bushes and standing up in a clearing like a green cave inside the forest. She could not see her feet. Her legs had disappeared almost up to the knees in creepers.

All was silent except for the thumping of her heart. It sounded like a drum inside her chest.

Quickly she tore off a strip of wild banana leaf in the way her mother had shown her when they had found the bush of yellow berries beside the stream and had no basket in which to carry the fruit home. She twisted it into the shape of a horn with a wide opening at the top, and pinned the leaf in place with a long white thorn from the African plum bush.

Her hands were trembling with haste. The rich, ripe, red plums dropped off at her touch, some of them falling down into the dark-leafed bush before she could catch them. Soon the twist of leaf was filled to the top.

All of a sudden, a branch above the bush moved. Tombi stared up in alarm. She looked straight into two black eyes, gleaming down at her. She opened her mouth to scream, but no sound came.

"ISIQUQUMADEVU!" she said in terror.

Then the eyes moved. A big hairy body came swinging across to another branch near her. With a loud chatter it scrambled up the trunk of the tree and disappeared into the leafy

jungle above. It was only a monkey!

Tombi clutched the twist of plums in her hands and, not caring about the scratches, crashed through the bushes back to the road.

The noise she made sent four large gray hadedahs flapping up into the air "Haa haa aa-ha-ha! Haa haa aa-ha-ha!" they cried as if they were laughing at her.

Gasping and panting, Tombi began to laugh, too, as she ran up the road. There was no such thing as the bearded monster. Fancy being frightened of a story like a very small child!

When Tombi reached the stall on the main road Zenela was still there.

"Tombi!" she called. "I have sold my basket for fifty cents and I have been waiting for you." Then she looked surprised. "But where is your sugar?" she asked.

Tombi told her and she exclaimed "Hawu!" for it was truly a dreadful thing to have dropped the sugar. "I shall stay to help you sell your fruit for not all visitors love African plums as much as we do."

There were still many cars on the road. Some of them stopped at the stall. The bigger girls crowded round, waving their bunches of bananas and their avocado pears. The women pressed forward, holding out their baskets and beadwork.

"See! See! See!" they all cried. "Bananas! Avocado pears! Baskets! Beads!"

Zenela and Tombi pressed forward, too. "Plums! Sweet red plums!" But the people in the cars could not see them behind the others.

"I am too small, Zenela," said Tombi sadly. "I am too small to sell fruit."

Then another car pulled up and a lady and a man got out. The man laughed and waved his hands to chase away the children. "No! No! No!" They only wanted to buy beads.

It was growing cold now. The sun had lost its warmth and a chilly breeze set the grass on the hills flowing like water. Tombi shivered in her cotton dress. Had she gone into the forest all for nothing? Would no one buy her sweet plums? Would she have to go home without money and without sugar?

Slowly and sadly and very softly
Tombi began to sing.
"Tula umntwana!
Hushaby baby!
Mama's coming!
She's gone to the store
To buy brown porridge."
She swayed and moved her legs. It
made her feel warmer when she
danced so she sang and danced a little
faster. She lifted up one foot and
with a twist of her body brought it
down again with a stamp. Then she
lifted the other foot. "Dance, Tombi!
Dance!" called the women who were
still sitting in the grass weaving.

They put down their half-finished
baskets and began to clap their hands
in time to the tune. They all liked to
see a child dancing.

"Dance, little Grandmother!"

Tombi laughed. She forgot she was feeling sad. Already her own special song was making her feel better. She swayed and twisted and stamped till the plums jumped up and down in the wild banana leaf and some of them landed on the ground. And she did not mind being teased. She could see now they were only teasing her because they liked her.

"Dance, Tombi, dance!" cried Zenela.

Then suddenly Tombi saw that the man and the lady were no longer buying beads. They were looking at her! She stopped at once and stared down at her feet. How could she dare to dance in front of strangers!

Zenela tugged her arm. "Tombi! The lady says she likes your Zulu dance. She says you must dance some more."

Tombi bent her head lower. She laughed into her hand but was too shy to go on. When she dared to look she saw that the lady was smiling.

"Thank you for your sweet, pretty song and dance, little girl," the lady said kindly. She pressed something into Tombi's hand and climbed back into the car.

Tombi opened her hand and gasped in amazement. It was a shiny coin!

"Twenty cents!" Zenela exclaimed excitedly. "Tombi! What you say is true. You are not a small child. You have earned some money!"

All the women laughed and talked at once, telling each other how Tombi had earned her money. They told the story over and over again, dancing and singing to show how Tombi had danced and sung. They were very excited and pleased.

Tombi could hardly believe it, but

there was the money in her hand.
Now she could buy some more
sugar!

"I must go to the store," she said.

"I will go with you, young sister,"
said Zenela. Then her dark eyes
laughed as they always did and she
added, "For it is getting late and
surely you will be afraid of ISIQU-
QUMADEVU."

Zenela was teasing her as if she

were a small child! But no, thought Tombi, Zenela teases me as the big people tease me, because she likes me. Then a thought struck her that made her eyes dance with even more merriment than Zenela's.

"I do not believe you about ISIQUQUMADEVU," she said, almost bursting with the laughter she was hiding inside herself.

"Oh so!" said Zenela.

"I believed you this afternoon and what you told me was wrong."

"How is that?"

"You told me that money was slippery. But you were wrong. It was the sugar that was slippery. Pshew! One minute it was on my head and the next it had slipped away!"

Zenela threw back her head and

laughed. Tombi laughed, too. They laughed and shared out the plums and teased each other all the way down the yellow sand road to the trading store.

Tombi did not even look at the dark forest for she was no longer afraid. Now she was a big girl. She had bought groceries and she had gone into a dark forest on her own and she had earned precious money. And best of all—now Zenela was her friend!

PRINTED IN U.S.A.